BEST STORIES

FOR

FIVE YEAR OLDS

Also available from Hodder Story Collections

BEST STORIES

FOR

FIVE YEAR OLDS

BY JOAN AIKEN
KAREN WALLACE
DAVID SUTHERLAND
JOYCE DUNBAR
GEOFFREY PATTERSON
JENNY ALEXANDER
KATHY HENDERSON
AND ANN TURNBULL

Illustrated by Katy Rhodes

First published in Great Britain in 1995 by
Hodder Children's Books

A Catalogue record for this book is available from the British
Library

ISBN 0340 646330

Typeset by Avon Dataset Ltd, Bidford on Avon, Warks B50 4JH

Printed and bound in Great Britain by
Cox & Wyman Ltd, Reading, Berks.

Hodder Children's Books
A Division of Hodder Headline plc
338 Euston Road
London NW1 3BH

Contents

Petticoat Palm

Joan Aiken

Petticoat Palm

Joan Aiken

When Joe went to stay with Grandma Quex the sea amazed him. For where Joe lived, the sea was grey and flat, and it lay dull and sad, on the other side of a grey, flat, stony beach.

But where Grandma Quex lived the sea was blue and clear, the colour of ink, and it roared and thrashed, in sheets of white foam, at the foot of a green grassy and black rocky cliff.

Grandma's palm tree stood on the top of the cliff and waved its fan-shaped branches wildly,

3

as if it were sending messages to the tossing sea.

"Of course I have to take great care of it," said Grandma. "It is *much* too far north for a palm tree to be growing. But your grandfather planted it and I'd hate to lose it."

A date in her diary every six months was ringed with red ink and the letters DOT.

"That stands for Department of Trees," said Grandma. "They think my palm tree is so important that they send a man every six months to make sure I am looking after it properly."

Joe didn't see how you could look after a palm tree. But one morning the radio weather forecast said, "There will be severe ground frost tonight in northern counties, even in coastal areas. And the wind chill factor will make it even colder."

"My gracious," said Grandma Quex. "And it's this evening that the DOT man makes his call. You'll have to help me, Joe. We must wrap up the tree."

Grandma Quex had a big old stone house, which stood sheltered in a dent of the cliff. The top floor of the house was all huge attics, which held junk and treasures and mysteries from past times, going back hundreds of years.

4

"These things will do to wrap up the palm tree," said Grandma, opening trunks in one of the attics. And she pulled out petticoats and pantalettes and a huge quilted crinoline, as big as an air balloon. And she pulled out shawls and chemises and shirts, she pulled out vests and waistcoats and wigs and wrappers.

"Fetch out the kitchen steps, Joe," she said, "and we'll do this job properly."

Grishkin, Grandma's cat, sat watching them all through the afternoon as they wrapped and dressed the palm tree. He thought they had gone mad.

By the end of the afternoon there was not a single inch of the tree to be seen. They had wrapped up its furry, webby trunk in petticoats and crinolines. They had pinned shawls and wimples and yashmaks and cloaks and plaids and mantles over its fan-shaped branches.

Joe thought the tree looked terrific.

"If only it could dance," he said.

"Now the DOT man can come just as soon as he likes," said Grandma. "But I'm worn out. I'm going in to make a cup of tea."

The Evening Star came out while Joe was standing on the cliff, admiring Grandma's palm tree in its fancy dress.

"Star light, star bright," said Joe, "first star I see tonight, I wish I may, I wish I might, have the wish I wish tonight. I wish that palm tree could dance."

No sooner were the words out of Joe's mouth then off danced the tree, tweaking itself out of the ground and capering down the steep hill as if it were happy to be set free at last!

"Hey!" bawled Joe. "Hey! Come back! You can't go off like that!"

But the tree paid no attention. Where it had stood was a deep hole, and something flashed at the bottom. Joe reached down and grabbed whatever it was, then he set off at top speed after the palm tree.

He was panting and gulping and horrified.

Somehow the palm tree had to be stopped, had to be brought back and set in its place, before Grandma came out and saw what had happened, before the DOT man came on his visit of inspection. Or he might say that Grandma was not fit to be in charge of a palm tree.

The palm tree went dancing and skipping down the cliff path. It seemed quite drunk with joy. It bounced, it whirled, it leaned from side to side.

"One thing," thought Joe, "we tied those clothes on really tight, Grandma and I. At least they aren't coming off."

Joe had a piece of chalk in his pocket. He drew arrows on the path, in case Grandma came out, to show where they had gone.

Luckily at the foot of the cliff path there was a big puddle of water, where the waves had splashed over.

The palm tree stopped to admire its reflection, and Joe was able to catch up.

"Please, tree, go back where you belong!"

But the tree danced on down the path.

Now they came to a kissing-gate, a wishing-gate, which was the entrance to the cliff path. The gate was like a stubby wooden cross, set

on top of a post, and you pushed it round in order to go through. The palm tree edged its wrapped-up shape past the first arm of the kissing gate.

And Joe cried out:

> "Gate, gate, wishing-gate
> Grant my wish, please don't wait
> Please, please co-operate
> Save my Grandma from disgrace
> Put the palm tree in its place!"

The palm tree cocked its branches to one side as if it was listening. Then it spun through the kissing-gate – all the way round – and went dancing back up the path, as fast as it had danced down.

Joe went panting after, rubbing out the chalk arrows as he went.

And when he got back to Grandma's house, he saw the palm tree jump into its hole and settle down with a shrug and a wriggle and a twitch.

Oh well! it seemed to be saying. I had a run. And I did have fun.

And it slipped in not a moment too soon, for there was the DOT man, coming up the road in his red car, and here was Grandma coming out of the old stone house.

"Well, sir!" she said proudly. "We've got our tree nicely wrapped up, as you can see!"

"You have indeed!" said the tree man. And he walked round the tree, admiring it.

Joe had a moment's horrible fright. Where was the cat, Grishkin? Could he possibly have been down in the hole, sniffing about, when the palm tree hopped back into place?

But then, with a huge gulp of relief, Joe saw Grishkin rubbing in a friendly way against the garden gate-post.

"No," said the tree man, walking round yet again. "The way you've got that tree snugged up, I reckon it should be good for another hundred years. And I'd not say no to a cup of tea, Mrs Quex!"

They all went inside for a cup of tea. And Joe pulled out the shiny thing he had put in his pocket.

"Why!" said Grandma. "Where in the world did you pick that up? Your grandfather's watch, that's been lost since I was a young girl . . . ?"

La Belle Lulu Labelle

Karen Wallace

La Belle Lulu Labelle

Karen Wallace

Once there was a little girl called La Belle
Lulu Labelle. She lived with her mother
and father and a big white poodle called
Patrick.

Lulu had thick black hair and eyes as brown
as chestnuts. Her mother would look at her
and sigh. She sighed because Lulu never
brushed her hair, hardly ever changed her
clothes and never ever wore a dress. Lulu
wasn't interested in things like that. She only
wanted to be with Patrick.

Every day Lulu made Patrick a new clip-on bow tie for his collar.

Every day Patrick walked with Lulu to school. When she went swimming, he watched from the gallery. When she did her homework, he lay under her desk and kept her feet warm.

One evening Lulu came down to supper. Her shirt was ripped and muddy. Her hair looked like a bird's nest. On the table was a snowy cauliflower in cream sauce with buttered peas and fresh green beans.

Lulu sat down. "I hate vegetables," she said. "Patrick doesn't eat vegetables. Why should I?"

"Ooh, la, la, Lulu!" cried Mrs Labelle, rolling her eyes and wringing her hands. "Whatever next?"

Her father twitched his moustache. "Patrick is a dog," he said. "Dogs don't eat vegetables."

Lulu pointed her chin at the ceiling. "Then nor shall I," she declared. "I shall eat only bread and cheese."

So the next day Lulu ate bread and cheese for breakfast, a cheese sandwich for lunch and cheese on toast for supper.

It was the same the next day and the day after that.

It was the same the next week and the week after that.

"Don't you get fed up with bread and cheese?" asked her friend, Jeanette.

"No," said Lulu. "I like it." She smiled and Jeanette noticed something rather strange.

Lulu's front teeth seemed to have grown and her ears were strangely furry.

That night Lulu didn't sleep in her bed. She decided she didn't like her pretty patchwork quilt.

Instead she curled up inside a large pile of leaves she had hidden in her cupboard.

The next morning Lulu had a piano lesson. As she sat down on her stool, the teacher's eyes popped out of his head. A grey tail was hanging from the hem of Lulu's skirt! As she played, it twitched in time to the music.

That afternoon Lulu had an art lesson and she painted a picture of herself.

When the teacher saw it, she jumped onto a chair and screamed.

It was a picture of a mouse.

"I'm sorry to inform you that your daughter has turned into a mouse," said the headmaster.

"What shall we do?" cried Mrs Labelle.

"Take her to the vet," said the headmaster.

"No child of mine goes to a vet!" shouted Mr Labelle. "She might catch fleas in the waiting room. I shall take her to a doctor immediately."

The doctor examined Lulu.

He counted her whiskers.

He measured the length of her tail.

He shone a little torch in her furry ears and felt the sharpness of her long front teeth.

"She is definitely a mouse," he said.

"Ooh, la, la!" cried Mrs Labelle, rolling her eyes and wringing her hands. "What can we do?"

"She must have no more cheese," said the doctor sternly. "She must eat only vegetables."

"But I like being a mouse," said Lulu. "I always win at hide and seek and if I don't like my lessons, I squeeze underneath the floorboards." She pulled a piece of cheese from her pocket and nibbled it.

Then she scampered from the room.

It didn't matter what kind of vegetables Mrs Labelle cooked. It didn't matter whether they were raw, fried, steamed or roasted.

Lulu would not touch them.

After a while, Mrs Labelle gave up. She got used to sweeping the leaves from her daughter's cupboard instead of making her bed.

She even cut little holes in Lulu's trousers so her tail would be more comfortable.

Mr Labelle gave up, too. He used to read Lulu fairy tales. But she didn't like them any more. None of the princes and princesses were mice.

So he read her mouse adventure stories and changed the endings so the mice always won.

As for Patrick, he spent his time lying alone outside the back door.

Lulu didn't make him bow ties any more.

He never went to school with her. And when she was at home she was too busy making nests in the sofa or looking for crumbs on the kitchen floor to play with him.

She even stopped swimming.

"Mice don't swim," said Lulu, firmly.

One day, Lulu was lying in the garden chewing

apple pips and admiring her tiny curled nails.

She didn't take much notice when the cat next door sat down beside her.

Then he moved closer. Suddenly she could smell his hot fishy breath.

Lulu's mouse heart went Pop! in her chest.

THAT CAT WANTS TO EAT ME! she thought to herself.

As fast as she could she ran across the garden.

The cat ran after her.

"Help! Help!" shouted Lulu. But because she was only a mouse, her shout was barely a squeak.

The cat was just behind her when she stumbled in the grass. "Someone help me!" she sobbed as she hit the ground with the tiniest of thuds.

Outside the back door, Patrick pricked up his ears and bounded across the garden.

Just as the cat opened his mouth to gobble Lulu up, Patrick jumped on top of him!

Lulu lay on the ground and howled. "I don't want to be a mouse any more," she cried. "I want to be a girl again." Patrick howled, too. He was unhappy because she was unhappy.

Mrs Labelle ran out from the kitchen. She

picked up her tiny daughter and kissed her furry pink ears.

"Ooh, la, la, Lulu," she said, gently. "Don't cry."

The doctor was right.

After a week or two of eating only vegetables, Lulu changed back into a little girl.

On the evening the doctor pronounced her completely better, Lulu came down to supper. She was wearing a brand new dress and her hair was tied up with a green ribbon.

"Ooh, la, la, Lulu!" cried Mrs Labelle, clapping her hands. "How lovely you look!"

On the table was a snowy cauliflower in a cream sauce with buttered peas and fresh green beans.

Lulu sat down. "I love vegetables," she cried, helping herself to a big plateful of everything.

"And what about Patrick?" asked her father with a twinkle in his eye. "Does *he* like vegetables?"

"He loves vegetables, too," replied Lulu Labelle, grinning.

And sure enough, there was Patrick, lying under the table and chewing on a carrot.

The Trouble with Anteaters

David Sutherland

The Trouble with Anteaters

David Sutherland

Max had an anteater but he soon found that it ate other things as well. One day it ate his mum's earrings. It wouldn't have been so bad if she hadn't been wearing them at the time. She was fairly upset.

The anteater was called Lenny and Max loved him terribly. They did lots of things together, like going for bicycle rides, playing frisbee in the park or going to the cinema. Some days they went to visit Max's Uncle Harold. Other days they went to the zoo to visit Lenny's cousins.

The only thing Max didn't like was when Lenny kissed him.

Anteaters, as you may know, kiss in the same way as dogs, only more so. Their tongues are not only *very* long, but also *very* sticky and slobbery. Of course, Lenny didn't understand that people don't normally like being kissed by a giant, hairy, Venezuelan anteater; he just happened to be very affectionate.

He liked to give Max a big kiss every day when he got home from school. He kissed Max's dad when he came home from work. He kissed Max's mum usually when she least expected it. (You must remember that an anteater can kiss from more than five feet away – even around corners!)

Max's dad got especially cross at times. He didn't like being covered in anteater slobber after a hard day at work. "Lenny, you horrible beast!" he'd shout. "Do that again and I'll cut your tongue off!" But of course he never did.

When it was Pet Day at Max's school, all the other kids came with their cats and dogs and hamsters, but he was the only one with a giant, hairy, Venezuelan anteater. Max brushed his black and white coat until it shone. "Please try to behave yourself for once," Max asked him.

"And don't go kissing Miss Dorrington or you'll be sent home!"

Everything would have been fine if Julia Fitzsimmons hadn't brought her Ant Farm.

An Ant Farm is essentially a bit of earth stuck between two pieces of glass with ants in it. You watch them walking around in their tunnels underground and it can be quite interesting – that is, if you like ants.

Well, it just so happened there was someone present who liked ants very much.

Everyone sat in a circle with their pets. Julia Fitzsimmons was directly across from Max. Lenny couldn't take his eyes off the Ant Farm.

Suddenly, without warning, he shot out his tongue! *SPLATT!* He hit the glass from across the room. Again and again he tried, but he didn't get a single ant and he couldn't understand why. Everyone laughed and Lenny looked very confused and disappointed. "Lenny's stupid," said Julia Fitzsimmons. "Doesn't he realise that he can't eat the ants through the glass?"

Everyone laughed again. Everyone except Max. He knew Lenny wasn't stupid at all. "He's probably a lot smarter than you'll ever be, Julia Fitzsimmons," he whispered to himself.

No sooner had he said this than Lenny

wriggled out of his arms and pounced across the room. Thinking she was going to be attacked, Julia Fitzsimmons shrieked and jumped back. But Lenny wasn't interested in her.

He knocked over the Ant Farm with his front paws. The glass smashed to bits and suddenly there were hundreds of ants everywhere! What a treat! Lenny lapped them up greedily with his long sticky tongue.

"Stop him! Stop him!" shouted Julia Fitzsimmons hysterically. "He's eating all my lovely pet ants!"

By the time Max could pull him away, there were hardly any ants left. Poor Julia was in tears. "Max," cried Miss Dorrington, "I think perhaps you ought to take Lenny home. He's done quite enough damage for one day!"

As soon as Lenny heard Miss Dorrington say his name, he simply had to give her a big sloppy kiss. He kissed Julia Fitzsimmons too, to thank her for the nice lunch, even though she had called him stupid. He was very happy.

Max was not very happy. On the way home, he told Lenny off. "Why are you so naughty all the time? You'll never win the 'Best Behaved Pet' award like that you know!"

But that afternoon things went from bad to

worse. The vicar had come to have tea with Max's mum. They sat on the sofa in the living room, talking about the church fête the following week. Max got on with his homework. Lenny was asleep on the carpet.

Max was vaguely aware of the sound of a fly buzzing around the room, but he took no notice. The vicar, a kindly man called Wilfred Dribble, was busy talking to Max's mum and he took no notice either – even when the fly landed on his nose.

But Lenny heard the buzzing, even in his sleep. He opened one eye and spotted the fly straight away. Without even raising his head, he shot his tongue out across the room. *SPLATT!* A bullseye! Poor Vicar Dribble didn't know what had hit him! He shrieked and flung his tea cup into the air and Max's mum had to jump to avoid getting scalded! Accidently she knocked over a lamp, which smashed down on the mantelpiece, sending two glass vases and an antique clock crashing to the floor!

Lenny calmly swallowed the fly and licked his lips as if nothing had happened. Max covered his eyes in despair, peering out at the wreckage between two fingers.

"Lenny!" his mum screamed. "Out of this house right now! OUT!"

Poor Lenny slunk away, not even realising what he'd done wrong. Max put him out in the garden.

"Lenny," he said, "that's the second disaster you've caused today! First you ate all Julia Fitzsimmons' ants and just now you nearly gave the vicar a heart attack! You can't go eating flies off people's noses like that. It's not polite. You're a bad anteater!"

Lenny looked up guiltily and gave Max a big slobbery kiss. *"YUCK!"* cried Max, wiping his face on his sleeve. "And stop kissing everyone all the time! If you don't stop misbehaving, Dad will sell you to the zoo!" Lenny looked at Max with his tiny black eyes and turned his head to one side. Then he scampered off and zapped a big ant on the garden wall.

When Max's dad came home that evening, he heard all about the disaster in the sitting room and he was not best pleased. "Max," he said sternly, "this has gone on long enough. Anteaters simply do not make very good house pets. Lenny has got to go."

This was the worst possible news. Lenny was his best friend in the world! Max knew his father was right, but it made him terribly depressed. He couldn't imagine visiting poor

Lenny at the zoo! He thought of him living in a cage, being stared at day after day by a lot of dumb tourists. It was unbearable!

That evening Max couldn't get to sleep. He lay awake for hours thinking about everything that had happened. Looking out of the window, he could see Lenny lying fast asleep in the garden.

"Sweet dreams, Lenny," Max whispered. "Who knows where you'll be this time tomorrow . . ."

He lay in bed with his eyes open, staring at the ceiling. It was very late. The house was dark and silent. His parents were fast asleep. Only Max was awake; awake and thirsty. Finally he got up and went down to the kitchen to get a drink.

The stairs creaked. Max's shadow crept along the wall beside him. He always found it exciting and a little bit scary going downstairs at night when everyone else was asleep, but he made it to the kitchen and got a drink of water without even turning on the light.

Putting away the glass, he turned around. He took one step, then suddenly – he bumped straight into a strange man with a mask! There was a burglar in the house!

They both jumped back. It was impossible to

say who was more startled! Max screamed and the burglar dashed past him, out of the kitchen door and into the garden. By this time, Max's parents were awake and rushing down the stairs to see what all the noise was about.

Max ran to the kitchen window and shouted, "Lenny! Get him Lenny! Don't let him get away!"

The burglar sprinted across the garden, preparing for a great leap over the back wall. But just as he jumped – *ZAPP!* Lenny's laser-quick tongue shot out and caught him by one leg! The burglar crashed to the ground and Lenny sat on his head so he couldn't move until the police came.

The police sergeant was very impressed. "That there beast deserves a medal if you ask me," he said. Lenny completely agreed and gave the policeman a big sloppy anteater kiss to say so.

Max's dad was pretty impressed too. "You won't sell him to the zoo now, will you Dad?" Max asked hopefully. "Lenny can stay now, can't he?"

"Oh, I guess so. But just make sure he behaves himself!"

"Did you hear that, Lenny?" Max asked. "You can stay! But you've got to be good! Understand?"

Unfortunately, Lenny didn't understand a thing. But everyone seemed to be pleased and that made him happy. So he gave Max's dad an enormously slobbery goodnight kiss and scampered up the stairs. He curled up on Max's bed and instantly fell fast asleep, dreaming about . . . What do you think? Ants, I suppose!

Queen Isabel

Joyce Dunbar

Queen Isabel

Joyce Dunbar

Let me tell you about Isabel. She might have seemed like an ordinary little girl but Isabel had a secret.

Really, she was a QUEEN!

How did she know she was a queen?

After all, she had no crown, only a squashed sun hat and a woolly bobble hat and a hood on her cagoule.

She had no throne to sit on, only a bean-bag chair to call her own.

She had no palace and no servants, only an

ordinary house with an ordinary mother and father. She had no one to rule over, except a baby brother called Timmy and a cat, and they didn't count because they wouldn't do as she said.

She didn't even have a Kingdom, just a long thin garden with a cherry tree that never grew any cherries.

But still, she knew she was a queen.

It was a feeling, deep inside her, that somehow she was special, that she was the *middle of the world.*

"When did the world begin?" she asked her mother.

"Oh, millions and millions of years ago, before you were born."

"What was it like?" asked Isabel.

"I don't really know," said her mother. "There were dinosaurs and—"

"Did you like the dinosaurs?" asked Isabel.

"I don't know," said her mother. "I wasn't around to see them."

"When will the world end?" asked Isabel.

"Not for ages and ages," said her mother. "Not for millions and millions of years. Now I must go and give Timmy his bath."

So Isabel talked to Ted.

"When I am queen, we can do as we want.

We won't let the world end, will we Ted? Not ever, ever, ever!"

Isabel practised being a queen. She put on her cloak, which was a curtain of shiny brocade, and made herself a paper crown. She tried to teach Ted to walk backwards.

"That's what you do with queens, Ted. When you leave the room, you mustn't take your eyes off a queen."

But Ted couldn't walk backwards. He couldn't walk at all but just kept falling over.

"Ah, but when I am queen, Ted, you'll be able to walk and *talk* as well – and *I* shall be able to *fly*!"

Isabel knew the day would come when it would all be for real. The curtain would rise, the bells would ring and the announcement would be made:

"All hail Queen Isabel! Long live Queen Isabel."

And she would order a banquet, and a fireworks display, and cherries on the cherry tree in the garden. She couldn't wait for that special day! She hoped it would come very soon.

It did.

"It's a very special day for you soon, isn't it my girl," said her father one supper-time.

"Is it?" said Isabel.

"Yes," said her father. "Our little Isabel will be starting school! Look what I've got for you!"

He showed her a brightly coloured rucksack and a new packet of felt-tip pens and a pencil with a frog rubber on the end. Her mother gave her a lunch box. Isabel was kitted out with a new skirt and jumper, socks, shoes and shorts and pumps. Then her mother took her to see her new school which was a long way away, in the town.

"It's very big isn't it?" said Isabel, staring through the huge iron gates. "Will I get lost?"

"There'll be plenty of people to look after you," said her mother, "and look, there's a climbing frame for you to play on and a bell up there in the bell tower."

And Isabel knew. She knew that the school was really a palace. She knew that the rucksack would become a golden coach and the pencil with the frog rubber was a royal sceptre, and that soon she would be crowned.

The night before school she hardly slept at all. Her stomach was so full of butterflies! "I'm glad you're coming with me," she said to Ted. "I hope I'll be a good sort of queen."

Her mother watched from the school gates and left her to play in the playground. There were so many other children! Isabel didn't know a single one. Then the bell rang.

Bing-bong-boiiing.

The children rushed to stand in line. A bunch of them were pushing and shoving to stand in front.

"*I* should stand in front," Isabel explained.

"No, *I* should!" said a much bigger girl with ginger hair.

"Never mind," Isabel whispered to Ted. "This is all part of the act. It's just to try me out."

Then they followed the teacher into a big hall. The moment had come! There was a stage, and a crowd of chattering children.

"Shhhhhh! Children! Shhhhhhh!" said the lady at the front.

Slowly, slowly, the noise died down. Slowly the children settled.

"Good morning children," said the lady at the front.

"Good morning Mrs Brown," chanted the children.

"Now, I want you to listen very carefully – ' she began. "I have something important to tell you."

Isabel closed her eyes and held on to Ted. She felt dizzy. She didn't want to be a queen! She wouldn't know what to do! She wanted to go to the loo and didn't even know where the cloakrooms were! "Please, oh please, not yet," she whispered.

This time she was lucky. The lady at the front didn't say anything at all about queens. Instead she talked about the school and the playtimes and the lovely day they were going to have. Then a piano began to play and everyone sang a song. But it wasn't a royal anthem. It was a song about a blackbird that spoke. Isabel breathed a sigh of relief. She didn't have to be a queen just yet.

The teacher took them to the cloakroom. "And you're Isabel aren't you?" she said. "Look, this is your coat peg with your name on it."

Isabel handed her coat to the teacher to hang up, just like her mother did at home. She wondered if the teacher would curtsey.

She didn't. "Oh no, Isabel," she said. "You hang your coat up yourself. And see, there are the toilets. Remember to wash your hands."

In the classroom Isabel was shown to a table which she shared with several other children. They didn't curtsey either; they took no notice of her at all. So Isabel took out her pencil with the frog rubber and her new packet of felt tips and she drew a picture of a queen . . .

. . . before she knew where she was, the bell was ringing again.

Bing-bong-boiiing.

The other children raced for the door. Only Isabel stayed where she was.

"Come back this minute!" said the teacher. "That is *not* the proper way to leave the room!"

Isabel knew what was going to happen. She had told Ted all about the proper way. The children would be made to walk backwards because they shouldn't take their eyes off a queen. But oh dear, no! She didn't want to be a queen just yet. "Please, oh please, not now," she murmured.

And once again she was spared. The teacher kept her secret! The children had to sit quietly and leave one at a time, then Isabel left too. It was all part of the act.

The day was full of hustle and bustle. There was a *bing-bong-boiiing* at mid-day and yet again no announcement was made. They all had lunch in the dining room. There was a *bing-bong-boiiing* in the afternoon and they all had a second playtime. In between they did all sorts of things. They played with the sand tray and in the wendy house and they made plasticine models. They painted and cut things out and stuck them down.

Yet Isabel was puzzled. If it was all part of an act, the other children played it very well – just as if it were real. They wouldn't even do as she said:

"I'll do the cooking," she announced in the wendy house.

"No, I'll do the cooking!" said a boy with rosy cheeks, snatching the saucepan off her.

Indeed, as the day wore on, Isabel began to wonder if she really wanted to be a queen. She sat in the book corner with Ted and had a word with him about it.

"You see Ted, I'll have to know where everything is, and the words of the songs, and what to order for lunch. And you see Ted, I can't even *read*. I'm sure that queens can read. Do you think I could change my mind and not be a queen after all?"

It was three o'clock. Isabel was tired. The other children were tired.

"Now children," said the teacher. "I want you all to put your things away on the shelves. You can see where they go. And then I want you to come and sit by me on the mat. This is a very special part of the day."

Isabel's heart beat faster. She held on to Ted. The teacher sat on a chair and all the children sat round her.

"Shhhhhh! Shhhhh! Shhhhhhh!" said the teacher. "Sit still, settle down, and be as quiet as you can. Then *listen*."

Some children still shuffled and whispered, but soon all was quiet. Isabel closed her eyes. The dreadful moment had come. All of the children would know. The world was a very big place and she was much too small to be a queen. She couldn't bear it for one moment longer. She jumped up, with Ted in her arms.

"I don't want to be a queen!" she wailed, and burst into floods of tears.

43

"Isabel! What's the matter?" asked the teacher, scooping her up onto her lap.

"I don't want to be a queen," sobbed Isabel. "I don't think I'm special after all."

"Of course you're special," said the teacher. "You're *all* special. But you can be especially special today Isabel and sit on my lap while I read a story to everyone."

And Isabel did.

And how special Isabel felt! And how she loved the story, about Barbar, the elephant, who wore a crown.

As the teacher reached the end of the story, the bell rang for the last time that day.

Bing-bong-boiiing. It was hometime.

That night Isabel had a long talk with Ted. "You don't have to walk backwards Ted, *never never never*, because I don't want to be a queen *ever, ever, ever*. I like being a little girl. There's only one thing Ted – the cherry tree in the garden. Now it won't ever grow any cherries."

But do you know, the very next year – it did!

Grandpa Fogarty and the Tangerine Shell

Geoffrey Patterson

Grandpa Fogarty and the Tangerine Shell

Geoffrey Patterson

"Do you believe in magic, Grandpa Fogarty?" asked Luke.

Grandpa Fogarty didn't answer, but stared out of the window at the sea.

Grandpa Fogarty had once been a sailor, but that was long ago. Nowadays, he spent most of the day combing the shore, peering through his pebble glasses at anything the tide might wash up onto the beach – usually shells that he would hold to his ear or, sometimes, driftwood that reminded him of some bird or

49

strange animal he'd once seen on his travels.

Grandpa Fogarty lived alone with his dog, Pip, except for a few weeks in the summer when Luke came to stay.

"Grandpa," Luke tried again. "Grandpa, do you believe in ghosts and things that go bump in the night?"

Silence.

"Grandpa Fogarty!" cried Luke, getting cross. "I'm asking you something!"

But Grandpa Fogarty ignored Luke's question and kept on staring out of the window.

"Please, Grandpa, do you believe in tiny voices that . . ?"

Grandpa Fogarty swung round. "No, I don't, you silly boy! What a load of rubbish! Tiny voices, indeed!" And with that, he stomped out of the kitchen into the garden.

Grandpa Fogarty was in a very bad mood, and Luke knew why. He had lost his Special Tin Box – the box that held all his most precious treasures: his brass compass, the penknife with the bone handle, the gold coin he had found on the beach, and the watch that chimed on a silvery chain. For one long year, Grandpa Fogarty had planned to give the Special Tin Box to Luke on the first day of his holiday. It was now three days since Luke had arrived and Grandpa Fogarty still couldn't remember where he had tucked it.

"We'd better see what *we* can do," said Luke to Pip. So, while Grandpa Fogarty was in the garden, they hunted high and low . . . on top of the chest, under the table, inside the cupboard, between the books . . . And, wonder of wonders, they did at last come upon it – behind the clock!

Luke and Pip rushed into the garden to tell Grandpa Fogarty the good news, but they caught him on the hop.

"Out of my way, you two!"

"Grandpa, you'll never guess!"

"Hang on, boy," said Grandpa Fogarty, "I've got to go in. I must catch the Weather Forecast!" And he pushed past Luke and went into the kitchen to switch on the radio.

"But Grandpa!, it's the —"

"You're not *still* going on about magic and tiny voices, are you?" bellowed Grandpa Fogarty. "Out of my way now, and *after* the Weather Forecast we'll go for a good, long walk!"

But Luke had a plan. There were over one hundred shells on the mantelpiece and he popped one of them into his pocket before tiptoeing out of the door. Outside, beyond the garden gate, there was a rock pointing like a finger into the sky. Luke put the shell – it was the colour of a tangerine – on top of the rock where Grandpa couldn't fail to spot it. Then he and the dog tucked themselves well out of sight behind the rock.

A moment or two later, Grandpa Fogarty stomped down the path, through the gate, and on to the beach, in search of Luke and Pip. Almost immediately, the tangerine-coloured shell caught his eye.

"Well, I never!" he said. *"That's* a beauty!" And he held it gently to his ear . . .

And the shell SAID something! It SPOKE to him in a little, tiny voice.

"Bless my soul!" roared Grandpa Fogarty. "I must be going crackers!" But he held the shell to his ear again.

And the tiny voice was still speaking: "Look behind the clock!" It whispered – "Behind the clock . . . the clock . . ."

"I *am* crackers!" muttered Grandpa Fogarty, but he pocketed the shell and stumbled back through the gate, up the path and into the house. And there it was – his Special Tin Box – behind the clock, just where he'd left it!

"Hooray!" cried Grandpa Fogarty, "I've found the Special Tin Box! Come and get your Special Tin Box, Luke!" Luke and Pip scampered gleefully into the house.

Grandpa Fogarty gave his grandson a big hug and threw the dog a bone to celebrate! "I hope you'll both forgive me for being so grumpy this morning. I thought I'd lost it for ever!" So saying, he handed the Special Tin Box over to Luke.

"Of course we will!" said Luke, sneaking a look at all the familiar treasures. "And thank you, Grandpa Fogarty, very much."

An hour or two later, Luke and Pip and Grandpa Fogarty were sitting cosily by the fire, enjoying their cocoa and biscuits.

"Grandpa, I must ask you something," said Luke. "*Do* you believe in magic and ghosts and things that go bump in the night . . . and tiny voices and things like that?"

Then Grandpa Fogarty, smiling broadly, gave Luke the answer he had been waiting for all day.

"Yes, Luke, I think I *do*. I do believe I do!"

Boris the Birthday Bear

Jenny Alexander

Boris the Birthday Bear

Jenny Alexander

"It's no good!" said Boris. "I'm not coming out!"
Benjamin peered into the darkness under the
bed, where the old bear was hiding.

"Come on, Boris," he said. "You can't stay
there all day. You'll miss your party."

"That's why I'm hiding," said Boris. "I hate
parties!"

It was Boris's birthday. He was seven, which
is quite old for a teddy. He had lost half
an eye, and most of his fur. One of his ears
was a bit chewed, and one of his paws was

crooked. But Benjamin loved him.

"What do you mean, you hate parties?" Benjamin asked. "Parties are great fun!"

"I'm sure they are – if you happen to like lying face down in a bowl of jelly for two hours . . ."

They both remembered Boris's second birthday.

"That was ages ago," Benjamin said, at last. "All your other parties have been fun."

"Oh, yes!" Boris agreed. "If you happen to like having your arm ripped off in a game of Ring o' Roses."

They both remembered his third birthday. Benjamin frowned. It looked as if Boris was going to have one of his grumpy days.

"All right, then," he said. "So we've had a few accidents. But last year's party was fun, wasn't it?"

"Great fun," said Boris, "if you happen to like setting fire to your nose!"

"Oh, yes," said Benjamin, remembering. "Well, I'll blow your candles out for you this time, OK?"

He reached under the bed, but his arm wasn't quite long enough. The tips of his fingers touched Boris's leg, but he couldn't grab hold of it.

"It's no good!" said Boris. "I'm not coming out!"

"Have you found him, yet?" Sarah asked, putting her head round the door.

Sarah was Benjamin's sister. She was twelve years old, and nearly grown up. She peered under the bed, too.

"Doesn't he want to come out?" she said.

She knelt down beside Benjamin and reached under the bed. Her arm was much longer than his.

"Come on, Birthday Boy," she said, grabbing hold of Boris, and pulling him out.

Boris gave her one of his fiercest looks.

"It's no good looking at me like that," she told him. "It's your birthday, and you've jolly well got to enjoy it!"

"Yes," added Benjamin. "And besides, Mum's already made the cake."

Every year, Mum made a teddy-shaped cake for Boris. It was dark chocolate brown, like he used to be, before his fur fell out. It had a red cherry nose, and two brown chocolate-button eyes, not broken.

"It's Boris in his young days," she said. "I'm afraid I can't do grey icing!"

"Who shall we invite to his party?" Benjamin asked.

"No-one," said Mum. "He's too old for a party."

"Thank goodness someone around here has some sense!" thought Boris.

But Benjamin was very sad.

"I know what!" said Sarah. "He could have a trip instead. Trips are great fun!"

Boris groaned.

"I'm sure they are," he said, "if you happen to like having your ear chewed off by a hungry raccoon!"

"That was your own fault," Benjamin said, "for jumping out of my back-pack. And anyway, it doesn't have to be the zoo."

"How about the fair?" said Sarah. "That's great fun, too."

"I'm sure it is," said Boris, "if you happen to like being dropped from the top of the big wheel, and having your eye broken in half!"

"That was your own fault, too," Benjamin told him. "You shouldn't have been leaning out."

"The play park, then," said Sarah. "You can't get safer than that."

"Oh, yes," said Boris. "That's great fun, if you happen to like having all your fur rubbed off, going down the slide!"

Mum laughed.

"Oh, my! Isn't he grumpy today?" she said.

"But never mind – we can't have a trip anyway, because it's raining."

"Thank goodness someone around here has some sense!" thought Boris.

"But we could go for a swim!" Sarah cried.

Boris fell off the table in alarm.

Gently, Mum said, "Boris doesn't like swimming. He's too old and worn out. Just look at him!"

"What do old, worn out people like, then, for a treat?" Benjamin asked.

He had an idea.

"I know! A day at the farm. That's what you had, isn't it, Mum?"

"That was a health farm, Benjamin. It's different," said Mum.

"A health farm," said Benjamin. "What's that?"

"A health farm is somewhere you go to relax," Sarah said.

Boris thought that sounded just the ticket!

"And people fuss over you, and feed you good food, and make you feel great," Mum added.

"Yes, yes!" thought Boris. "That's for me!"

Dad came in from his early morning jog.

"What's going on?" he asked.

"We're going to turn the house into a health

farm today, for Boris's birthday treat," Mum told him.

"Right!" said Dad. "Then we'll need to start with a Computer Profile. Come on, Benjamin."

Dad helped Benjamin make a picture of Boris on the computer. He put in the chewed ear, the broken eye, the crooked arm, and the bald back and tummy.

Then Dad typed out a list of things Boris would need, to make him feel as good as new:

1. Warm soapy soak.
2. Sauna.
3. Brush and rub.
4. Healthy dinner.
5. New ear and eye.
6. Stitch on arm.
7. New fur.

"That should do it," said Dad.

So Benjamin ran a bath for Boris. He put in lots of bubbles. And Boris had a lovely long soak.

When Boris was all clean, and fairly dry, Benjamin looked at the list again.

"How do we do a sauna?" he asked his dad.

"We put Boris in the airing cupboard for an hour or so, and let him steam gently."

After that, Benjamin rubbed Boris's floppy arms and legs, and brushed what was left of his fur. Then they all had carrots and cottage cheese for dinner.

After dinner, Benjamin and Sarah raided the biscuit tin – healthy food didn't seem to have filled them up very much!

Mum repaired Boris's ear, and gave him a new eye. She put a few stitches in his arm, to make it straight.

They all looked at the list. There was only one thing left – new fur. How on earth were they going to do that? But Sarah had spent the day making Boris a new body wig, out of a piece of red fur. He put it on.

He looked wonderful! He felt fabulous! Boris jumped up onto the table, and did a little dance.

"I feel as good as new!" he cried. "Come on, everyone – let's have a party!"

But Benjamin and Sarah and Mum and Dad all groaned. They were quite worn out!

The Very First Blackbird

Kathy Henderson

The Very First Blackbird

Kathy Henderson

Some things are true and some things are stories. And sometimes things that sound like stories turn out to be true after all. It's hard to know.

Jim was a little boy who used to wake up in the night quite often. He'd lie there in the dark and think things or hear things. And sometimes he'd get scared. Then he'd tiptoe to his mother's room.

"There's something there," he'd say.

"Hmmm," she'd mumble, mostly asleep, "What?"

"A rustling" it would be one night.

"A banging" another.

"Elephants!" said Joe one middle of the night when she didn't want to hear.

And usually he'd curl up in her bed and warm his cold feet on her and go back to sleep that way.

But one night, no, very early morning, almost dawn with the first blackbird just starting to sing in the dark, Jim came into his mother's room again.

"I heard something!" he said.

"Hmmm," she mumbled as she always did, mostly asleep. "What?"

"I don't know. A sort of scratching."

"Hmmm," said his mother and she rolled over to make room for him as usual.

But Jim didn't want to get in.

"There's a noise, Mum. Come and listen!"

"Noise," she sighed, putting the pillow over her head.

But Jim wouldn't give up. No. He lifted the pillow, he pleaded and tugged until, in the end, his sleepy mother stumbled up out of bed and along the passage to Jim's own room. She flopped down on the bed and yawned.

Jim's room was just starting to shake off the night. Its clean white walls were coming out of the shadows now and the square shapes hanging on them were turning back from dark holes into pictures. A mirror and a chair reappeared, and a bookshelf with books and tapes and bears and cars, and then two big toy boxes and a cupboard. The first pale light of the early summer sun came creeping in round the edge of the curtains and more birds sang outside. It was peaceful and safe and as quiet as could be.

Jim's mother lay down on his bed and pulled the duvet up over her.

"Aaah!" she said, all cosy, and closed her eyes.

"No Mum, listen!"

They both listened . . .

And heard . . .

Nothing.

Except the first early morning city rumbles, dozy noises, car grumbles, door slams, a nee-naw in the distance, the wind ruffling things and more and more birds singing.

"I can't hear anything," mumbled Jim's mother snuggling her head further into his pillow, three-quarters asleep again already.

"There *is* something there!" said Jim, "I *know* there is!"

He froze. She dozed.

Scrabble! went something.

Jim's mother opened her eyes.

Scrabble! Cheep! went something again.

She sat up.

"See?" said Jim shivering. "There's something there! It scrabbles. It cheeps. It could be a rat! It could be a monster! . . . It could be . . ."

What could it be?

Jim and his mother looked for the noise.

They drew back the curtains and let the light pour in and then they looked all round the room.

They looked into the cupboard,

and under the bed,

through the bookshelves

behind the books and the tapes and the bears round the toy boxes among heaps of furry things and don't-throw-those-aways

and they couldn't find that cheeper anywhere.

They pulled back the covers and riffled through the clothes. They looked outside the windows and behind the door. They looked into and onto and under and over everything until there were only walls and floors and ceilings left and they couldn't find that noise at all.

Cheep! Peep!

Jim's mother sat down on the bed again and cuddled Jim up next to her.

"Don't worry," she said, "we'll just have to listen harder and see if we can hear where it's coming from."

"*Zheep!*" it went again.

Jim pointed to the top of the wall opposite. His mother pointed to the bottom of the cupboard next to it.

"Over there."

"But where?" They crept over to the place and waited again.

Scrabble. Cheep!

This time it was so loud they both jumped.

"It's in there!"

75

"But that's the wall!"

A cheeper in a wall?!

A zeeper in the bricks?!

Jim's mother looked hard at the smooth white wall.

"See that?" she said, and she pointed to six little slits not far up from the bottom. "That's an airbrick. They put them in walls to let air into hollow places. I think there was a fireplace here once and someone's covered it up. And where there's a fireplace there's always a flue, like a tunnel that goes up to the chimney pot so the smoke can get out." She looked at Jim and she wasn't at all sleepy now.

"You know what?" she said. "I think something's fallen down the chimney and into the place where the fireplace used to be behind your wall."

Scrabble. Scrabble went the noise.

"A rat?" asked Jim, shuddering.

"More like a bird," said his mother.

"Can't it get out?"

"No, it's trapped. We'll have to get it out . . . Or it'll die."

"Quick!"

"I know," she said and she got up to leave the room.

"I'm coming with you," said Jim, scuttling

after her quickly. He didn't want to be left behind. Not with a chimney, a fireplace, a hole and something trapped, all behind his quiet white wall! No thankyou!

Cheep!

Down the stairs to the kitchen went Jim's mother, pulling on a sweater and some socks on the way. Down the stairs to the basement. She dug around and found a hammer and a chisel and a screwdriver and some old newspapers and then came all the way back to Jim's room again with Jim running alongside, carrying things.

Zheep!

They could hear it from the top of the stairs. "Hurry!" said Jim.

Cheep! Scrabble!

Together Jim and his mother pushed the furniture out of the way. He spread out the newspapers on the floor. With one hand his mother pressed the chisel into the wall next to the airbrick, with the other she took the hammer and hit the handle of the chisel hard with it. The clean white wall cracked. A chunk of plaster fell out onto the floor. The cheeping stopped.

BANG! TAP! CRASH! CRUNCH!

Jim's mother chipped and chopped round one

side of the airbrick, two sides, three sides and four until *BANG CRASH!* she pulled the whole brick out in a cloud of crusty dust and soot and grit.

There was silence.

Jim and his mother looked into the hole. It was dark in there, very dark. Nothing moved. There wasn't a sound.

Very carefully Jim's mother put her hand into the hollow space behind the hole and felt around.

"I can feel something," she said. "It feels like feathers. It feels quite big. I think it's a bird. But it's stiff . . . It's cold . . . Oh dear," she took her hand out. "I think it's dead."

Jim and his mother sat there on the newspaper full of broken plaster and sooty dust and looked at the wrecked wall and the messed up room. All that to rescue a bird and now it was dead! Jim felt like crying. It was very quiet.

Suddenly there was a whirling and a scrabbling and a shower of soot.

Cheep! Zheep! Cheep!

A very small dirty bundle of panic-stricken feathers whirled out of the hole and past their heads. It flew round and round bumping into the walls and crashing into the lampshade.

The noise seemed loud as thunder. The room seemed small as a cage.

Jim jumped back. His heart was pounding. "It's alive after all! But it'll hurt itself!"

"Quick! Shut the door so it can't get lost in the house!" said his mother and she ran to the window and threw it open.

Round and round, banging and fluttering *Cheep! Zheep!* flew the dusty little bird until, at last, at last, it flew out of the open window and away into the summer morning, leaving a trail of soot, and Jim and his mother quivering.

"I don't understand," said Jim's mother, "I thought it was dead. I'm sure it was dead. I'm glad it wasn't."

"Did we rescue it?" asked Jim.

"Yes. I think we did."

Jim's mother went back to the hole in the wall and started tidying up the mess.

"It doesn't really make sense," she said, looking puzzled. Jim watched her put her hand into the hole and feel around again.

"Ah!" she said. "Look!" and out she pulled a big bundle of black feathers. It was a dead blackbird she was holding, all dried up, just bone and feather.

"There were two birds, not one," she said.

This one must have fallen down a long time ago and nobody heard."

Jim took the dead blackbird and cuddled it. He looked into the dark hole and he looked out at the sky and he thought of the song that he sometimes heard when he was awake in the night before it was even light. The song of the very first blackbird high on the rooftops.

"Poor thing," said Jim. "Poor thing."

"I'll help you bury it when I've fixed your wall," said his mum, going to fetch filler and paint. "And then we'll have to get someone to come and cover the chimney pot with wire so that no more birds can fall down there."

They buried the stiff dead blackbird in the garden. Jim was sorry to see it go into the ground.

He wondered what else lay behind the skin of the house and his mother wondered which things were stories and which were true.

Shadow

Ann Turnbull

Shadow

Ann Turnbull

Shadow lived in Bill's garden, but she was not Bill's cat. She was a stray cat, shy of people.

It was Bill who named her Shadow.

"Because you're so quiet and secret," he said, "and yet whenever I turn round, there you are: my shadow cat."

"I'm not your cat," said Shadow.

But she liked to be near Bill when he was gardening. Sometimes she dozed in the catmint, with the sun warm on her fur; sometimes she kept cool under the laurel bush;

sometimes she watched the frogspawn twitching in the pond. If Bill was digging she would come and scratch in the crumbly earth.

But she would not let Bill touch her. She hissed if he came too close. Shadow was shy of people, even Bill.

"I don't know what you live on," said Bill.

He put out food and milk for Shadow, near the back door. Shadow drank the milk and ate the food and licked the plates clean, but although Bill always left the door half open, she never came in.

"You need somewhere to go when it's raining," said Bill.

He opened a window in the shed so that Shadow could slip inside.

By day the garden was Bill's; by night it was Shadow's.

"I wonder what you do all night," said Bill.

Shadow looked at him with round gold eyes. She said, "I watch the moon through a net of leaves. I fish for stars in puddles. Mice go skittering through the grass and turn to dry leaves in my paws. Strange cats come. I stare them out; stare outstare till they slink away. This is my garden. No cat hunts here but me."

Spring turned the garden green. Daffodils

bloomed. Frogs hopped and splashed in the pond and Shadow splashed after them.

"Have to get planting soon," said Bill.

But then came snow: sudden snow that piled up deep drifts beneath the apple tree and under the rockery. The daffodils' petals were clogged, the pond sealed in ice.

Shadow hated the snow. It soaked her fur and stung her eyes. She lifted each paw in turn and shook it.

All night it snowed, and all the next day. Shadow went to the shed, but the catch on the window had dropped shut in the wind and she could not get in.

She sat under the laurel bush and waited.

In the evening Bill put out her food. Shadow ran to meet him.

"You're wet, lass!" He tried to stroke her, but Shadow shrank away. "Come on, then. Eat your dinner. I'll go back in the warm."

But he left the door open, just a crack. And when she had eaten, Shadow felt the warmth of the house calling to her. She put a paw on the door sill.

"Come in, Shadow," Bill said.

Shadow crept inside.

Her ears went back at the hiss of the gas fire, but its warmth was kind. She felt the hearth rug soft under her paws.

"I'm not a house cat," said Shadow, "but I will stay here tonight."

She listened to the ticking of Bill's clock and the creak of his chair. The sounds were comforting. She purred and fell asleep.

The next night Shadow came in again. This time she was bolder. She sprang onto the television and up to the mantelpiece and picked her way between the clock and the silver-framed photograph of Bill's wife, Margaret, and then down again onto the back of Bill's chair.

"Shadow," said Bill, "you're all alone out there, and I'm all alone in here. We could be company, us two."

Shadow looked at him with round gold eyes. She said, "I am not a house cat. My place is in the garden. I guard the pond where the star frogs leap at night; I know their hiding places under the lilies. I stalk birds at dawn and leave my paw prints in the dew. I don't need company."

But after that night, whenever the wind was cold or rain was falling, Shadow would scratch at the back door to come in. Then she would sit in the warm room with Bill and his television and the photograph of Margaret, and Bill would listen to her purring.

Shadow began to lose her fear. She let Bill stroke her. She rubbed her head against his knees. And one day she jumped on his lap and purred and plucked with needle claws.

Bill smiled and stroked her. "Everyone needs company," he said.